MARC BROWN

ARTHUR'S CHICKEN POX

Little, Brown and Company

Boston   New York   Toronto   London

For all the chicken pox experts in Mrs. Bundy's class at DeWitt Road School, with love and thanks!

First Paperback Edition

ISBN 0-316-11384-0 (hc)
ISBN 0-316-11033-7 (pb)
Library of Congress Catalog Card Number 93-22996

10   9   8   7   6   5   4   3   2
WOR
Published simultaneously in Canada
by Little, Brown & Company (Canada) Limited

Printed in the United States of America

It was Monday morning, but Arthur's family was thinking about Saturday's trip to the circus.

"I wonder if the knife thrower will be back," said Father.

"The trapeze artists are my favorite," said Mother.

"I like the clowns best," said Arthur.

"I like the cotton candy," said D.W.

Arthur thought about the circus in school, too.
For his art project, he drew a picture of the circus.
Then at lunch, Arthur noticed he didn't feel very well.
He went to the nurse's office.

"You have a temperature," said the nurse. Then Arthur's dad arrived to take him home. "I'm going to get better fast," said Arthur. "I don't want to miss the circus."

D.W. was surprised to see Arthur when she got home from
play group.
"What's wrong with you?" she asked. "You don't look sick
to me."
"But I *feel* sick," said Arthur.
"I think you're faking," said D.W.

At dinnertime, Arthur got to have chicken noodle soup on the sofa.

"Why do I have to eat at the table?" asked D.W.

"You're not sick," said Mother.

"Well, I think Arthur is just pretending," said D.W.

"Eat your spinach," said Father.

The next morning, Arthur was *really* sick.

"Arthur has polka dots!" said D.W., laughing. "Too bad he'll miss the circus."

"I'll see if Grandma Thora can stop by later," said Mother. "She knows all about chicken pox."

That afternoon, Grandma Thora arrived.
"I brought you some treats to help you feel better," she said.

After school, Arthur's friends stopped by with get well cards.
Muffy brought Arthur all his homework.

Father brought Arthur some stickers and cherry cough drops.
"Can I have a cough drop?" asked D.W.
"You're not sick," said Arthur.

"I feel all itchy," said Arthur after dinner.
"Try not to scratch," said Grandma Thora.

"But I want to scratch," said Arthur.
"I'll make a special soothing bath," said Grandma Thora.
"That might help."

Arthur was allowed to drink juice in the tub with a crazy straw. "If you're a good little boy and don't scratch your spots," said D.W., "I'll bring you home a balloon from the circus."

After his bath, Grandma Thora gave Arthur a back rub and told him a story.

"I think I'm ready for my hot tea now," said Arthur. "Don't
forget the extra honey! Please!"
"Can I have a back rub, too?" asked D.W.
"Maybe later," said Grandma Thora. "Right now I have to get
Arthur's tea."
Suddenly, D.W. got an idea.

She went to the bathroom and closed the door.

First D.W. put baby powder on her face to look pale.

Then she looked through her marker box for a pink one.

And she gave herself spots—lots of spots.

D.W. made loud moaning sounds as she came down the stairs.
"I don't feel well," she said.
"Good heavens," said Grandma Thora. "You have them, too!
Let me take your temperature."

When no one was looking, D.W. held the thermometer under hot water.

"Oh, dear," said Grandma Thora when she read the thermometer.

"I feel itchy, too," said D.W. "I think I need a soothing bath."

"Of course," said Grandma Thora.

"And how about some juice," asked D.W., "with a crazy straw?"

"Of course, darling," said Grandma Thora.

D.W. didn't notice that while she was in the tub, all her pink spots washed right off.

But Grandma Thora noticed.

"Dora Winifred!" she scolded. "I'm very disappointed in you."

"Well, how's our little patient?" D.W. asked Arthur the next afternoon.

"Still itchy," said Arthur. "And still sick."

"That's too bad," said D.W.

She moved the telephone near Arthur.
"Excuse me," she said. "I have to make an important call."
"Hello, Emily? I have an extra ticket for the circus on Saturday.
Want to go with me? . . . Great! Bye."
"Mom!" moaned Arthur. "D.W. is torturing me."

By Friday, Arthur was feeling well enough to go out to dinner with his family.

"I guess I'll be going to the circus after all," he said.

"Oh, that's just grand," said Grandma Thora.

"D.W., you'd better call Emily," said Mother.
"Maybe I should wait," said D.W. "Who knows? Arthur might get the flu."

But Arthur didn't get the flu.
The next morning, he was up early and dressed for the circus.
Everyone else was ready for the circus, too.

Everyone except D.W.

"Hurry up, D.W., or we'll be late," called Mother.

D.W. came down the stairs singing, "It's cotton candy I love to eat. It's so squishy. It's so sweet."

Mother just looked at D.W.
"Oh, boy," said Father.

"Good heavens," said Grandma Thora.
Arthur started laughing.
"What's so funny?" asked D.W.

"Back to bed, young lady," said Mother.
"But what about the circus?" cried D.W.
"Don't worry," said Arthur. "If you're a good little girl and
don't scratch, I'll bring you home a balloon."